# A LITTLE SCRIBBLE SPOT

Written & Illustrated
by Diane Alber

To my children, Ryan and Anna:
Art is one of the best forms of expression!

## This book belongs to:

_____

_____

_____

This is Scribble SPOT, and he doesn't look like he's feeling well...

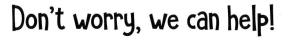

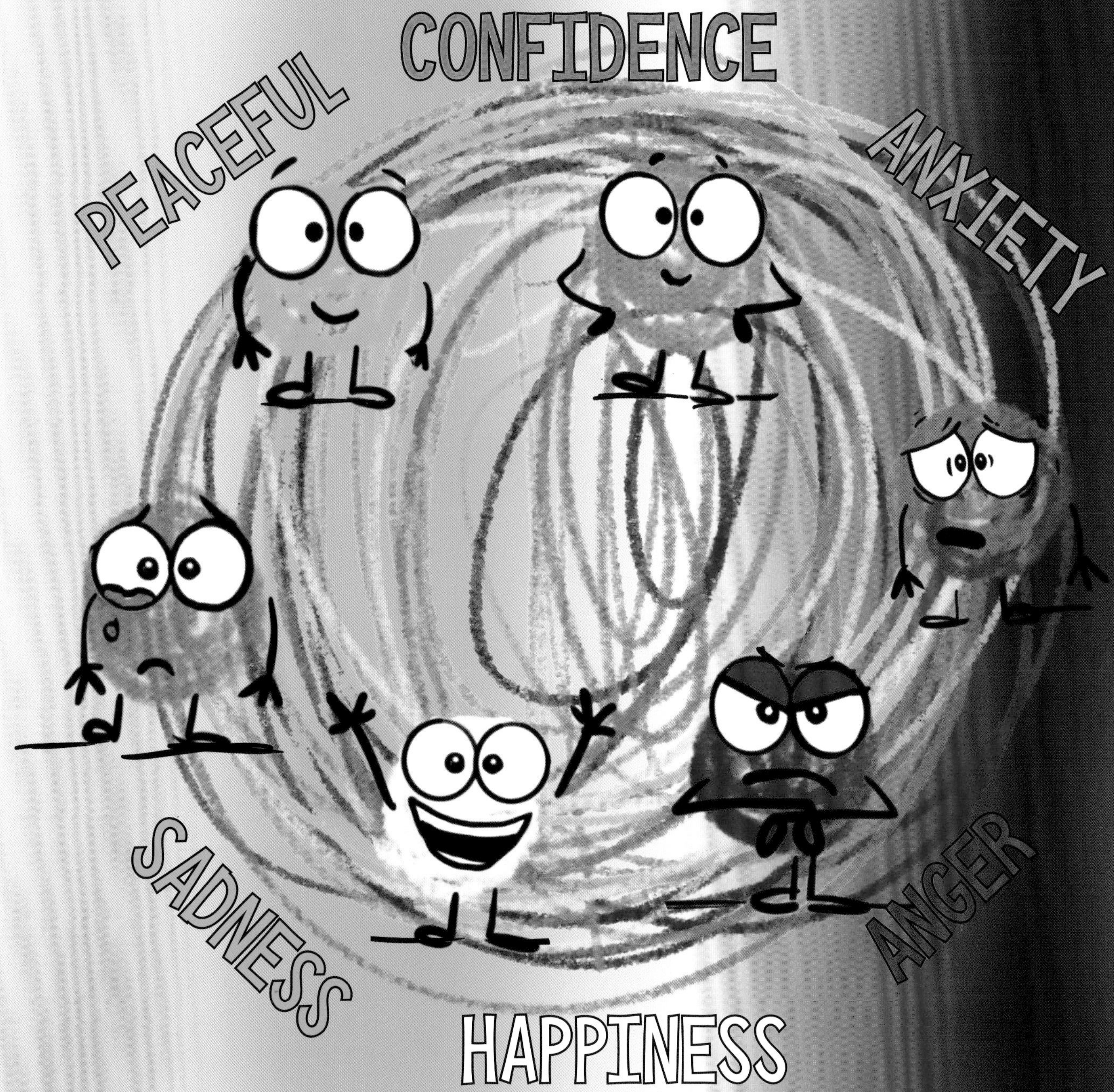
CONFIDENCE
PEACEFUL
ANXIETY
SADNESS
ANGER
HAPPINESS

RELAXED

QUIET

TRANQUIL

CALM

MELLOW

SERENE

PEACEFUL SPOT scribbles
TREES and VINES.

SADNESS

INVISIBLE

FORLORN

LONELY

FORGOTTEN

SADNESS SPOT scribbles
GLOOMY CLOUDS and TEAR DROPS.

PLEASED

ECSTATIC

MERRY

CHEERFUL

GLAD

HAPPINESS SPOT scribbles
SUNSHINE and FLOWERS.

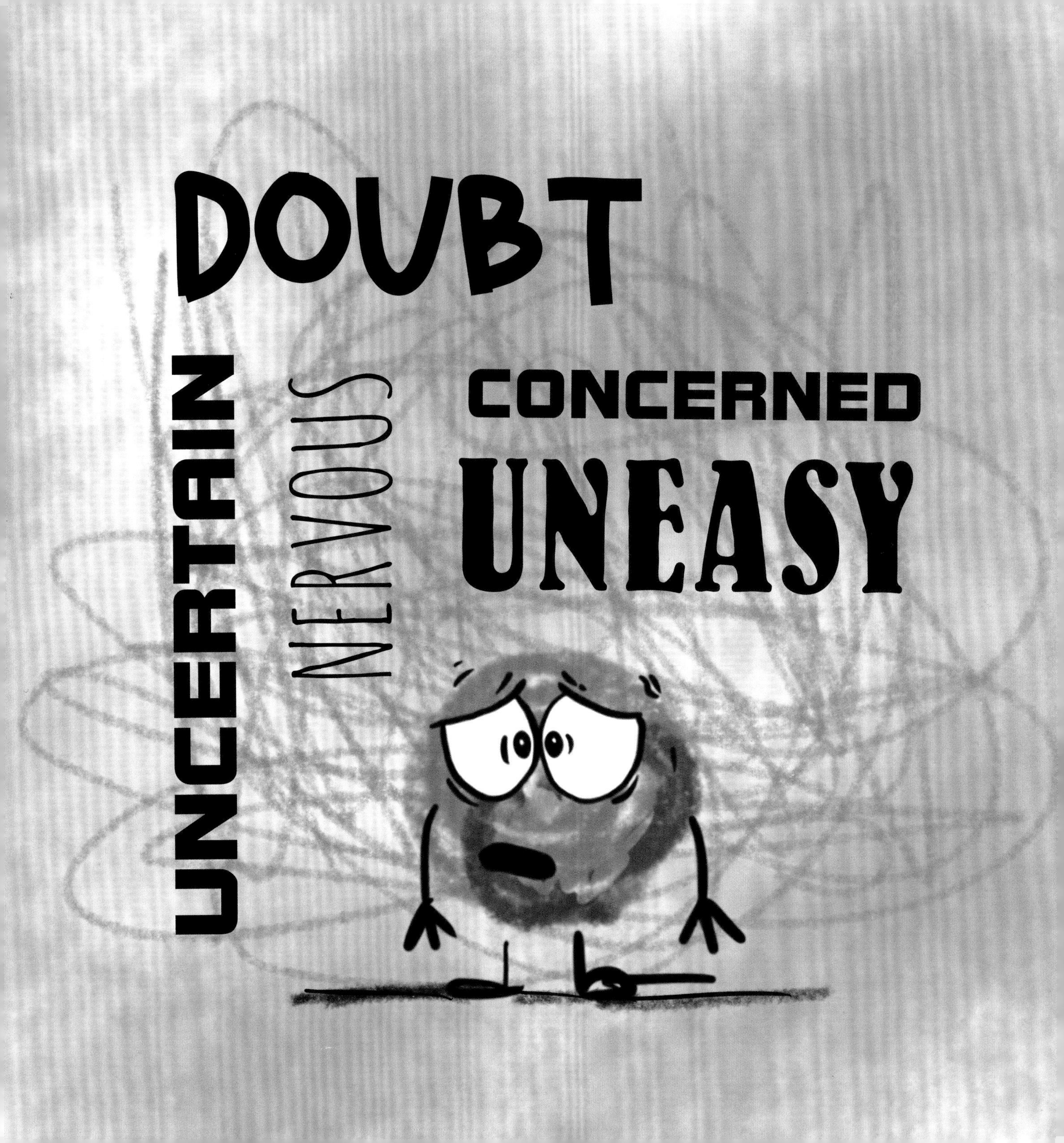
DOUBT
UNCERTAIN
NERVOUS
CONCERNED
UNEASY

ANXIETY SPOT scribbles...

# NOTHING...

(He is worried it wouldn't look good.)

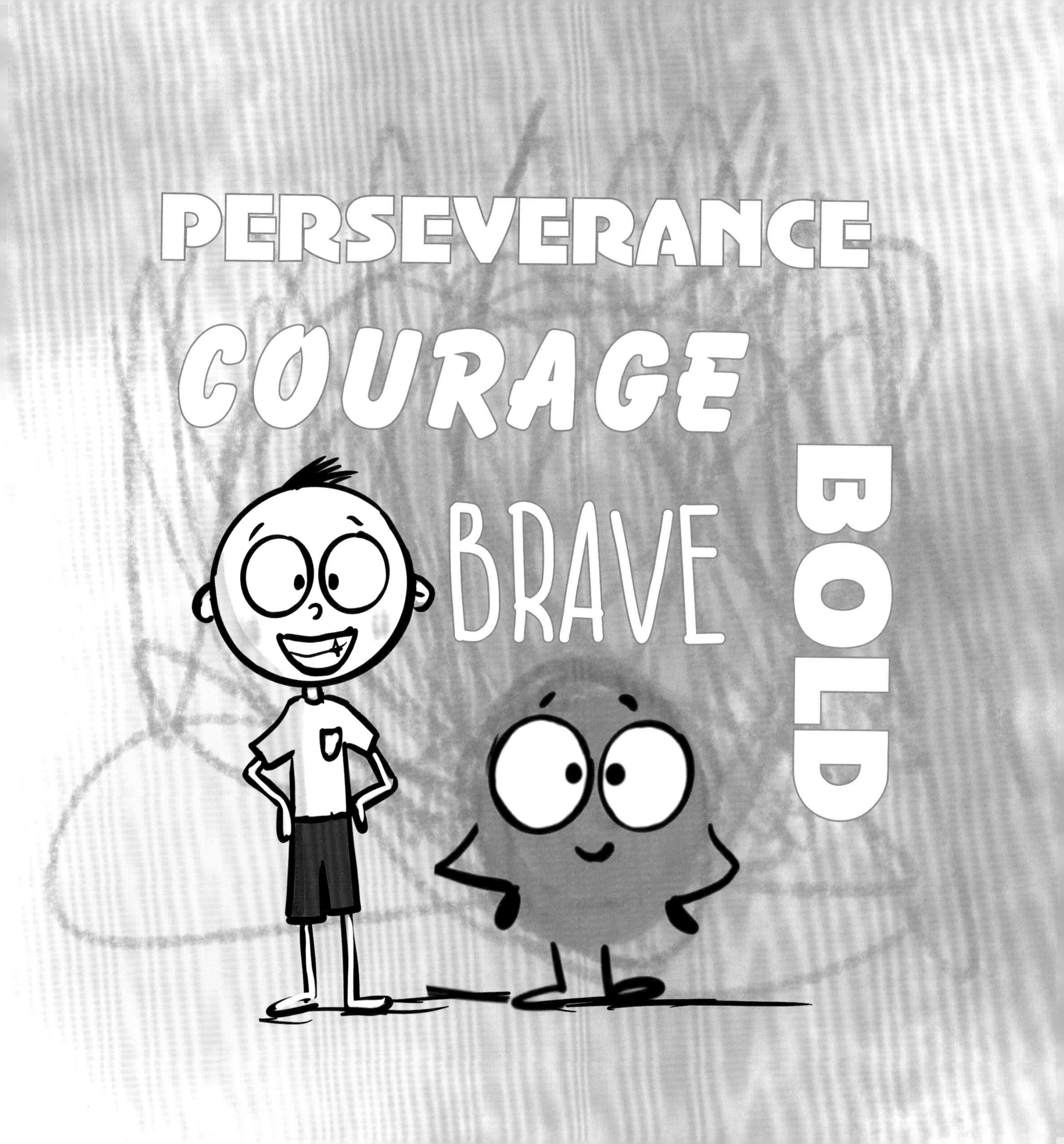
PERSEVERANCE
COURAGE
BRAVE
BOLD

CONFIDENCE SPOT scribbles
STRENGTH and DETERMINATION.

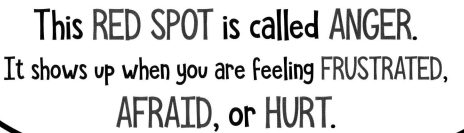

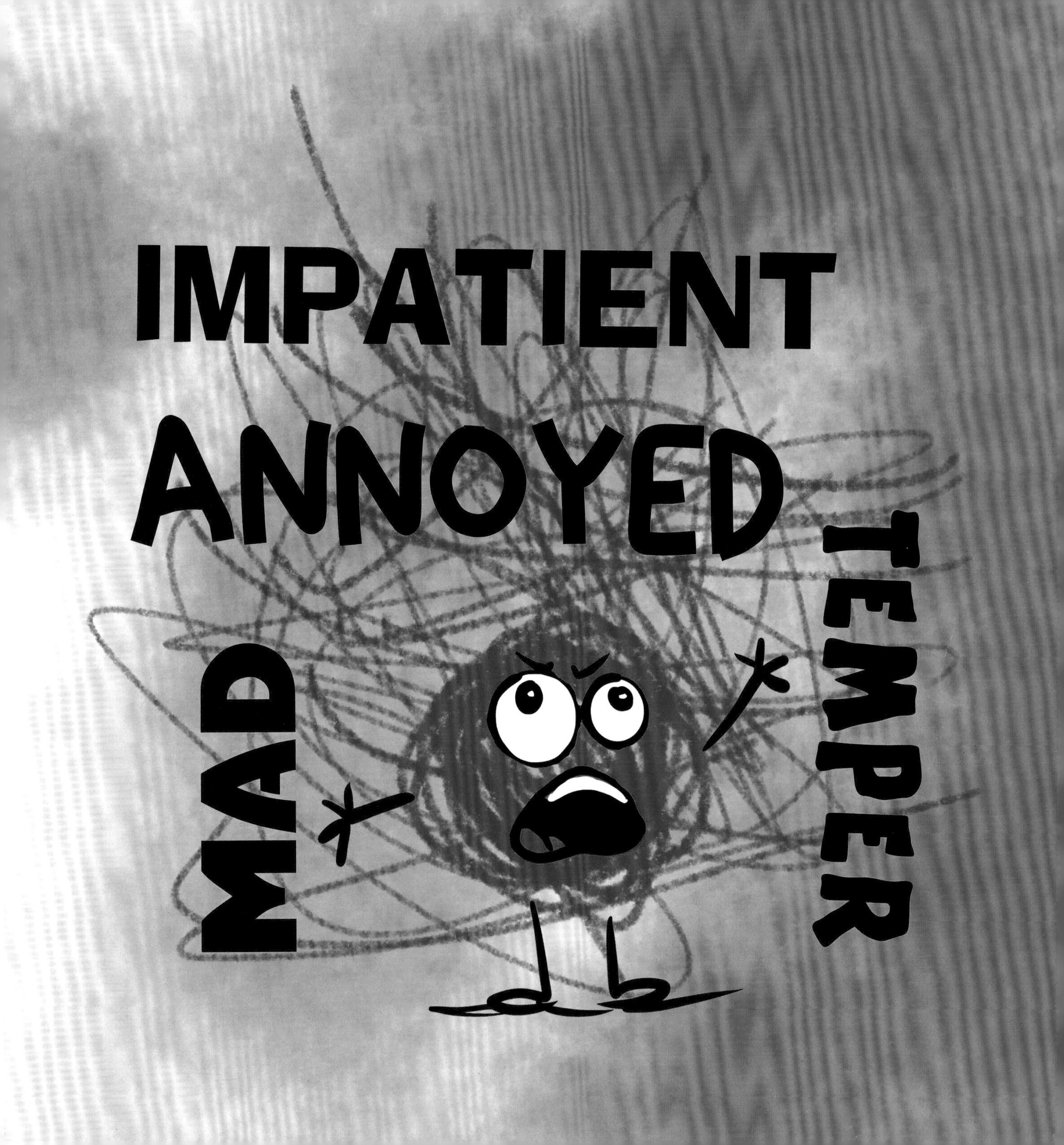
IMPATIENT
ANNOYED
MAD
TEMPER

# ANGRY SPOT scribbles...CHAOS?

I can't believe we forgot LOVE!
LOVE is made up of so many feelings and emotions. You experience LOVE when someone cares about you, or you care about them, A LOT!!

# SCRIBBLE SPOT scribbles a...
# RAINBOW!

Because every EMOTION is within us.

# From the Author:

Thank you so much for taking the time to read this book!
This story was developed to be an introduction to the various emotions we all feel every day.
When children start to feel BIG emotions, it can be challenging to show them how to manage their feelings in a healthy way. That is why I created the "Inspire to Create A Better YOU!" series. Each emotion is broken out individually to highlight specific examples and coping strategies that are easy to understand and apply to everyday life!

Diane Alber

   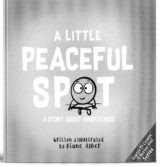

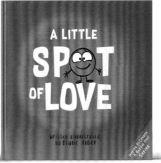 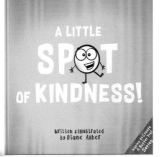 

Now grab a piece of paper and some crayons and scribble YOUR EMOTION!